Candy
Come Home

Also available in this series:

Candy
Come Home

Linda Jennings
illustrated by Kate Aldous

MAGI PUBLICATIONS

for Alex
LJ

for Alice
KA

First published in Great Britain 2002 by
LITTLE TIGER PRESS
1 The Coda Centre,
189 Munster Road, London SW6 6AW
www.littletigerpress.com

Text © Little Tiger Press, 2002
Illustrations © Kate Aldous, 2002

Kate Aldous has asserted her right to be identified as
the illustrator of this work under the Copyright,
Designs and Patents Act, 1988.

All rights reserved • ISBN 1 85430 845 9

A CIP catalogue record for this book
is available from the British Library

Printed and bound in Great Britain
by Bookmarque Ltd.
Set in 16.8pt Goudy

1 3 5 7 9 10 8 6 4 2

Contents

Chapter One

Candy and Spike were born on a cold, wet and windy night in early spring. The rain was falling like sharp needles, and the kittens had no real shelter – only an old cardboard box lined with newspaper which was squashed between two dustbins.

Mother Cat kept them warm as best she could and curled her body around them.

After ten days, Candy and Spike

opened their eyes. Mother Cat watched them carefully as they wriggled around their box getting to know each other, then took their first tentative steps into the world.

Very soon the kittens were old enough to play tag between the dustbins. They wrestled and tumbled and sometimes got quite rough.

"Come on, you two," said their mother. "There's no need to fight."

Soon their mother's milk was not enough for them. The food from the bins was mostly not suitable for young kittens.

"Mice are best for you," said Mother Cat. "I'll have to go out to hunt. Stay hidden, little ones. There's lots of danger out there."

The kittens didn't listen to her. As soon as she was gone, Candy and Spike chased and ran and jumped. There was a whole world out there, waiting to be explored!

"Bet I can climb that wall!" squeaked Spike.

"Bet you can't!" said Candy.

Spike scrabbled and clawed and heaved himself up, until he was wobbling on the very top of the wall. But it was an awfully long way down to the ground again!

"Help!" he squeaked. He was stuck.

"What *are* you doing up there, Spike?" Mother Cat scolded, when she returned later with a very small mouse. "You could have fallen off and hurt yourself."

She helped him down.

"Is that all?" asked Spike, looking at the mouse. "I'm starving."

Mother Cat sighed. "It's getting harder and harder to find proper kitten

food for you," she said. "And you are both too young to help me hunt."

Later, when the hungry little family curled up in their cardboard box for the night, Candy could not sleep. "I'm not too young," she thought. "I bet I could catch a big rat all by myself. And then Mum and Spike would think that I'm the cleverest kitten in the world."

She waited until Mother Cat's purr had faded to a soft snore and Spike lay sleeping with all four paws in the air. Then she crept out and made her way down the darkened street.

Chapter Two

The moon was high as Candy trotted to the edge of the village. It was all so new and exciting to her! Candy walked on and very soon came to a big, wooden barn. She poked her little head round the open door.

"Yuk, what a pong!" she said aloud. "It smells worse than our dustbins."

"It's the best smell in the world," boomed a deep voice. "A wonderful mix of horse dung and giant rat!"

Candy peered into the darkness. A big brown horse was looking down at her.

"Did you say *rat*?" squeaked Candy.

"Of course," said the horse. "The place is full of big, fat rats who would eat you for breakfast!"

"Oh no," said Candy boldly. "I'll eat *them* for breakfast. That's why I'm here!"

"LOOK OUT!" shouted the horse.

Candy looked, and all the fur on her body stood on end. For there in front of her were two enormous rats!

"B-but they've got big, sharp teeth!" squeaked Candy.

"Stay still," said the horse quietly. "Don't move a whisker."

And before Candy could blink her startled eyes, the rats went flying

through the air and landed on a
high hay bale.

"That was some kick!" Candy gasped. "Thanks so much."

"Don't mention it," said the horse, kindly. "But take my advice, you go right back home. This is no place for a kitten frightened of rats."

Candy managed to stop herself shaking. She took one big breath and ran from the barn as fast as her little legs could take her.

It was getting light as she drew near the dustbins. Candy hoped her mum would be asleep, then she wouldn't get told off. But the dustbins were empty and the cardboard box was no longer there. Neither were her mother or Spike.

Candy settled down to wait for them.

"Perhaps they're out looking for food,"

she thought. "I hope so. I'm really hungry."

Candy waited all day. At one point someone filled the dustbins again, and she hid a little way off, but she was soon back again. She didn't want to miss her mum and Spike if they returned.

She grew hungrier and hungrier, and more and more upset. At last, as night fell, she curled up on the hard ground in a tight little ball.

When morning came, Mum and Spike were still missing. What had happened to them? Perhaps they had abandoned her. But in her heart of hearts, she could not believe this.

"Well, there's no use hanging around any longer," she said. "I'll just have to start looking for them."

By now Candy was starving. She scrabbled up to the top of the dustbins, but they were only full of newspapers and empty tins. It was all very well boasting about catching rats, but she knew she must now hunt to survive. And since the dustbins didn't contain anything she could eat, she would have to move far away from her home. Carefully she washed herself from tip to toe, before setting out into the open countryside.

Chapter Three

The long day turned to night, and Candy's legs felt wobbly as she made her way across the fields towards the shelter of a wood.

"Well, I've seen healthier looking cats in the cemetery," called a fat owl from the branch of a tree. "Looks like you could do with some food to fill out your skinny little bones."

"I'm all right," said Candy. "I'm looking for my own supper."

"OK, suit yourself," said the owl. "Only, as I've caught more than enough for myself, I thought you might like to share."

Candy hesitated. "*Never speak to strange animals*," her mother had told her.

"After all," went on the owl, "I'm a

bit overweight and you're underweight, so it makes good sense."

It did, too. Candy gave in. Within minutes, she was busy tucking into the mice the owl had just caught.

"You've left one," said the owl.

"Yes, well, it's just in case I come across my mum and brother," said Candy, sadly. "I've lost them, you see. And I know they would just love a nice, juicy mouse."

"Poor little kitten," said the owl, kindly. "All on your own in the world. You'll have to learn to stand on your own four feet!"

"I will!" said Candy. And off she went to look for her lost family, taking the mouse with her. Very soon, though, she ate the mouse. "After all," she thought, "it won't keep fresh for my family."

Candy walked and walked until her little paws were red and sore. At last, she reached a riverbank.

SPLASH!

Startled, Candy stared. Some fish were leaping into the air, as if they were dancing.

"I could catch one of those!" Candy thought.

The next time the fish leaped, she jumped at one – and fell into the water!

The water swirled around her, as she was quickly carried downstream.

"Jump on to my back before the current drags you down!" called an otter.

Candy was too frightened to do this. Supposing the otter grabbed her and ate her? She struggled some more, but she had nothing to hang on to. She was getting tired, and finding it harder and harder to stay afloat.

Candy realised she had little choice, and so she agreed to let the otter give her a ride.

"Otter River Bus at your service," said the otter. "Goodness, you look more like a wet, scrawny bird than a cat."

He set the kitten gently down on the bank. "Cats can't swim. What were you doing in the water?"

"Trying to catch a fish," said Candy, washing herself frantically. "And now I'm hungry, tired and aching all over. But thank you for rescuing me."

"Think nothing of it," said the otter. "Why don't you come back to my home for something to eat?"

* * *

Candy stayed with the otter for several days. She told him all about her family, and how she longed to find them again.

"I had a family once," said the otter. "Brothers and sisters. We had such fun together. But they all grew up and moved away. You have to do your own thing in the end, you know."

"But I don't want to live alone," said Candy.

"Sometimes I get very lonely, too," said the otter. "Perhaps you would like to stay with me for a while longer?"

Candy thought about it. It would be fun, living with the otter. But she knew she had to leave. She had to find her family.

"Thanks a lot, Otter," said Candy. "But it's time I moved on."

"I'll miss you, little cat," said the otter. "But I do understand."

As she walked along the riverbank, Candy looked back.

The otter waved a sad paw from the water. "I hope you find your family," he called.

Chapter Four

The summer wore on, and Candy was no nearer to learning what had happened to her family. But it became easier for her to find food. The otter had taught her how to fish, and she was getting the hang of hunting for mice. Even so, she sometimes went hungry.

One day, as she was strolling through a wood, she heard a strange snorting noise. She stiffened.

What could it be? A friend or an enemy? She decided to be brave.

"Come out from there, or I'll come to get you, and then you'll be sorry," she called.

A badger poked his head out from behind a bush.

"Really?" he said. "And what will you do then? Tickle me to death with your tail? Hiss at me? Scratch both my eyes out?"

"I don't know why you find it so funny," Candy said, in a huff. She put her tail straight in the air and marched off down the path.

"I wouldn't go that way, if I were you," called the badger.

"Why not?"

"There's a fox about, and there's nothing he'd like better than a tasty young cat."

Candy ignored him. How dare he laugh at her!

"Please yourself," said the badger. "But if you do meet him, you need to run away as fast as you can."

Candy walked on. She could look after herself now, thank you very much!

Something rustled in the bushes.

"That old badger again," thought Candy.

SNAP! went a branch.

Something whined and slobbered. It didn't sound like the badger.

Too late, Candy realised it was the fox! Its red head poked out from behind a tree and it licked its lips. Its mean little eyes squinted at her.

"Well now," said the fox. "It looks like I won't have to travel far for my supper."

Candy froze. What was it the badger had said? *"Run away as fast as you can!"* But Candy was so frightened that she couldn't move.

"But I must," she thought and suddenly she ran for her life. The fox followed. Candy was now strong and full of energy, but the fox had longer legs. It got closer and closer.

Just in time, Candy noticed a hole in

the ground. She dived down it, and scrabbled through a tunnel. Then she collapsed, exhausted.

"Welcome to my sett," said the badger. "You should have listened to me in the first place."

The fox was whining and clawing outside the sett, but the badger soon saw it off. It slunk away, furious at losing its supper. Candy was still shaking from head to toe.

"Rest for a while," said the badger. "Then I'll show you around."

The badger's sett was amazing. There were dozens of tunnels, leading in all directions.

"Escape routes," said the badger. "Everyone should have an escape route. Remember that."

* * *

Candy stayed with the badger for several weeks. He taught her a lot: which animals were friends and which were not. But it took Candy a long time to get over her fright with the fox and she wouldn't venture out without the badger by her side.

"You'll have to learn to stand on your own four feet sometime," said the badger one day.

"That's funny," said Candy. "That's what the owl told me."

Candy was getting restless. She had to move on. She had to keep looking for her family. The next day, she felt ready to leave.

"Goodbye," said the badger. "I'll never forget you."

"I won't forget you, either," said Candy. "Or everything that you've taught me."

Chapter Five

It was colder now, and the days were getting shorter. One wet and foggy afternoon, Candy was walking down a lane when she saw a shadowy shape ahead of her. She stopped. What sort of animal was it?

The shadowy shape stopped, too.

"Oink, oink!" it said.

A pig! What was a pig doing in the middle of a lane? Come to think of it, it was a funny looking pig.

Suddenly, the shape hurtled towards her.

"Everyone should have an escape route," the badger had told her, and Candy looked frantically around.

The wall beside the lane was high, but she had no choice. Candy gave one enormous leap and landed on top of it.

She looked down into the fog. The pig was standing right underneath her, panting and whining. Except that it wasn't a pig at all. It was a big, shaggy dog!

"Hello," said the dog.

"Hello," said Candy cautiously. "It wasn't very nice of you to chase me."

"Dogs always chase cats. It's only natural. I wouldn't have hurt you, though."

"No?" said Candy. "Well, I'm not coming down to find out."

"That's a pity," said the dog. "Because you do look like you need a good meal and shelter. Come back home with me."

"Home?" said Candy. "Where is home?"

"My master has a caravan in the woods," said the dog. "He loves animals – even a mutt like me who can only make pig noises!"

"What's your name?" asked Candy.

"Guess," said the dog.

Candy tried to think back to her days living beside the dustbins as people walked by with their dogs on leads. What sort of names had she heard?

Rover?

Sam?

Rufus?

None of these seemed to suit the pig-dog.

"Piglet – what else?" said the dog, laughing.

"Well, he sounds friendly enough," thought Candy, "and I would like to find somewhere to rest for the night." She decided to risk it.

She jumped down off the wall and followed Piglet home.

In the twilight, the caravan looked very cosy, with smoke curling from the chimney and a lantern glowing outside. But Candy suddenly stopped.

What if it was a trap?

"If it's all the same to you, I'll sleep underneath the caravan," she said.

Candy explained to Piglet how she had lost her family in the spring, and had been searching for them ever since.

"What do they look like?" asked Piglet.

"My mum is tabby, and Spike has a black patch on his eye and his fur stands up in little tufts. That's why he's called Spike."

"Two cats passed by here a couple of months back," said Piglet. "Just like the ones you described."

Candy's heart lifted.

"Where were they going?" she asked.

Piglet shook his head. "They didn't stop to speak. They seemed to be searching for someone."

"Me," thought Candy. "They were looking for me."

"But the direction they were taking was towards the big town north from here."

Candy crawled underneath the caravan, and Piglet brought her out some chicken and a piece of cooked fish. She ate them hungrily, and settled down for the night.

Chapter Six

Piglet had explained to Candy exactly how to reach the big town. He had warned her, too, about how different it was from the country, and how dangerous. But over the months, Candy had learned a lot. She had learned how to survive. She wasn't afraid!

As she drew near Candy saw more and more houses and more and more people.

It was dusk by the time she reached the middle of the town.

Candy crouched in an alley. She was wary of the people coming home from work, and kept well away from their hurrying footsteps. Across the street, she could see a shop. A delicious smell wafted over to her. Fish!

Candy hadn't eaten since the night before. Her mouth watered as she saw a boy and a girl drop the remains of their fish supper into a litter bin.

Should she chance it? She stared out at the road, where cars and lorries flashed by. The temptation was too great.

"I can make it if I move quickly," thought Candy. Suddenly, there was a gap in the traffic, and she took her chance. She ran right across the busy road, dodging the oncoming cars.

Candy could hardly believe it. She had made it! Shaking in every limb, she crouched on the pavement, getting her breath back. What a lucky escape!

Just as soon as she had stopped trembling, Candy reached up towards the litter bin.

"Scram, cat!" cried a voice. "That's *my* supper!"

"Mine!" hissed Candy, standing her ground. She wasn't going to let her supper be taken so easily, after all that danger!

She turned to face her foe. It was a large ginger cat with a torn ear. He looked mean and tough.

"Take my advice," said the ginger cat. "You get out of here as fast as you can. This is no place for a little cat like you, still wet behind the ears."

"I'm not!" protested Candy. "I've lived alone for months. I've caught my own fish and mice, and I've faced up to a fox." (Well, that wasn't quite true!)

"I've walked for miles to get here and I'm not giving up now! I've been walking all day and the pads on my paws are nearly worn out."

"Don't tell me about sore pads," said the ginger cat. "Let me tell you my pads are sore, my legs are sore,

my back is sore! Life in a town isn't easy, you know."

Candy looked the ginger cat up and down. Tufts of fur were missing where he had been in fights, and he had lots of battle scars. But all the same, there was something in the old cat's eyes that Candy recognised as kindness.

"Perhaps we could share the supper?" Candy suggested.

"Why not? And you can crash down with me tonight, then go your own way tomorrow," he said.

Candy followed the cat home. He lived, as she herself had done so many months ago, in an old cardboard box squashed behind some dustbins.

As they settled down for the night, she told the ginger cat about her family.

"You haven't seen them, by any chance, have you?" she asked.

"Cats come and go," said her new friend. "But now you mention it, I do remember seeing a spiky looking cat with a black patch on his eye about a month ago. Raiding the dustbin, he was, and about your age."

Spike! Could it have been?

With all her heart, Candy hoped that it was.

Chapter Seven

The next morning, when Candy awoke, the ginger cat had already left. She sat for a moment, wondering what to do. The town was so big, and there were so many places to search. And the ginger cat had seen Spike ages ago – even supposing it had been Spike.

All the hope that Candy had felt the previous night faded away. Where would she begin to look?

"Well, I can only follow my nose,"

she thought. "It's what I've been doing for months."

Candy made her way down the street, flattening herself against the walls to avoid being trodden on. Then a child tried to grab her, and she dashed through an open door.

To her dismay, it closed after her, and she found herself in a brightly lit room full of flowers. She crouched by a bucket and tried to hide herself from the human who stood behind the counter.

"Well, what are you doing, little cat?" said the woman.

She sounded kind, but Candy was frightened of being grabbed, as the child had tried to do. She looked out through the flowers with big, scared eyes.

The woman walked towards her and knelt down.

"Puss, puss, come here."

Perhaps the woman would give her food and shelter and let her live in the bright shop amongst the flowers. But Candy knew she couldn't stay. She had never lived with humans before, and she needed to find her family.

Just as the woman tried to pick her up, the shop door opened and Candy shot out.

Candy ran and ran until she came to another part of town. It was quieter here, and there were trees and gardens. There were people taking dogs for walks on leads and cats sitting on garden walls, washing themselves. They looked sleek and well-fed. Candy felt a bit safer, and slowed down. Perhaps one of the cats could help her?

"Excuse me," she called to a slinky Siamese admiring its reflection in the gleaming metalwork of a car. "I'm looking for my mum and brother. I wonder if you've seen them? One is tabby with a white bib and one –"

The cat looked down its nose.

"Clear off, you scruff," it sneered. "Go back to your dustbin. We don't want the likes of you round here."

Poor Candy! She had always tried to look nice, even when she was starving. She had always groomed herself every day. How dare this snooty cat speak to her like that!

"Let me tell you," she said to the Siamese, "I've seen the world, which is more than you have. I've faced a fox, and nearly been drowned in a river. I've been chased by a dog who sounded like a pig. I've –"

The Siamese flexed its claws.

"Why, you cheeky young brat!"

"Stop it, you two!" A cat had jumped lightly on top of the car, and stared

down at Candy and the Siamese. "There's no need to fight."

Somewhere, long ago, someone had said just that to Candy. Someone who had scolded her and her brother when their many friendly wrestles had got a bit out of hand.

Candy stared up, and a tabby cat looked down at her.

"It can't be –" gasped the cat.

"Mum!" whispered Candy. "It is you, isn't it?"

The cat jumped down on to the pavement, cuffing the Siamese as she did so. It slunk away, with its tail down.

"Yes, it's me, my little kitten. Though you're not a kitten any longer. My, how you've grown!" She gently licked Candy on the ear. "I thought I would never see you again."

"I've been looking for you for ages," said Candy. "And I've had loads of adventures. But where's Spike?"

"Spike's here, too. We've found a lovely home. Come, I'll show you."

Candy followed her mum over a wall and into a garden. A cat was sharpening its claws against a tree.

Spike!

Candy ran towards her brother and they rolled over and over on the lawn. They cuffed each other, and wrestled and chased, just as they had done so many months ago when they had been kittens. Then they followed their mother through a cat-flap and into a little wooden shed.

Inside was a large cardboard box with blankets in it. And there were two saucers with just enough food left in them for Candy.

"The humans are good to us here," said Candy's mum. "We're wild cats at heart, so we don't stay in the house. But they feed us and make sure we're well and happy."

"Will there be enough food for three?" asked Candy.

"I'm sure there will," said her mum.

As they all curled up together in their box, Spike told Candy everything that had happened to them. How the dustmen had come one morning, and taken away their cardboard box, with Spike still inside it. How their mum had jumped on to the dustcart and been driven miles before she could rescue Spike. How both of them had escaped from the dustcart and found themselves on the edge of a strange town, a long way from their home.

"We set out each day to look for you," said Candy's mum. "But with no luck at all."

Candy told them of her adventures. She said she had never given up hope of finding them. She told them how she had learned to stand on her own four feet.

And when she had finished, she snuggled up to Spike, closed her eyes and purred with happiness.

For more information about books
from **Little Tiger Press** or for our
catalogue please contact:

Little Tiger Press
1 The Coda Centre
189 Munster Road
London SW6 6AW

Tel: 020 7385 6333
Fax: 020 7385 7333
E-mail: info@littletiger.co.uk

Or visit our website:
www.littletigerpress.com